Fairythorn Tales

by Lara Faraway

Posy and the Trouble with Draglings

templar

12522998

A TEMPLAR BOOK

First published in the UK in 2013

by Templar Publishing,

an imprint of The Templar Company Limited,

Deepdene Lodge, Deepdene Avenue,

Dorking, Surrey,

RH5 4AT, UK

www.templarco.co.uk

Text by Sara Starbuck
Illustrations by Jan McCafferty
Design copyright © 2013 The Templar Company Ltd
Scents copyright © Celessence

celessence™
Scent technology by Celessence™

First edition

MIX
Paper from
responsible sources
FSC® C020471
www.fsc.org

ISBN 978 1 84877 970 9

Printed and bound by CPI Group (UK) Ltd, Croydon CR0 4YY

Prologue

Our world is only the beginning. Beneath the surface and between the moonbeams there is another place. A place where the flowers sing and birds and animals live happily with the little people of Fairyland.

All the magic in our world comes from this place, through doorways that only the fairies can open. And, at the centre of the magic is the Fairythorn Tree.

The Fairythorn, as the little people call it, is always the oldest tree in any garden, wood or park. It might be gnarled and spiky on the outside, but it is a comfortable home for the tiny fairies who live hidden inside its trunk and branches.

And if you look very closely, right down where the base of the trunk meets the mossy ground, you might just spot a doorway to the fairies' world.

Look very closely, now. It's even smaller than you think…

Chapter 1

The Miller's back garden looked like a great, dark living room. The grass was a shaggy green carpet, the wild rose bushes looked like chunky armchairs, and a large, round moon hung in the sky like a gigantic lightbulb. It was the dead of night and everything seemed silent and still. But if you'd paid close attention, you might have realised it was neither.

The tiny little fairies from the

Fairythorn Tree and their even tinier draglings were flitting about all over the garden. As usual, they were very busy. Whatever the season, when you're a fairy and have Mother Nature to answer to, there's always a lot to be done before morning.

Posy, was standing on the shed roof, looking down over the garden like a sentry guard. The fairy narrowed her big green eyes and peered hard at a suspicious-looking shape near the house belonging to the humans – or Bigs, as the fairies called them. It was only a watering can, she eventually decided, but she knew she couldn't be too careful. Not with Grot Goblins about. And not when Mother Nature had specifically asked her to help keep watch.

Posy tied back her wild black hair into plaits and crowned it with a headdress that she'd made from peacock feathers and thorns. A small gold horn hung round her neck. Above her

head, Posy's constant companion, her pale green dragling, Dash, was circling slowly, keeping watch too.

In the garden below, Posy could see her best fairy friends, Rose, Honeysuckle and Fleur, helping the Dewdrop Fairies sprinkle water over the plants and flowers. It hadn't rained for days and everything was thirsty.

Fleur waved up at Posy as she swooped over the lawn on the back of a grey cuckoo. She was scattering water out of a tiny dolls-house teapot as she went. Her dragling, Red, was close behind, with a dripping wedge of soggy sponge clutched in his talons.

Honeysuckle was dancing on her tiptoes around a lavender bush, swinging a tin thimble on a rope of spider's thread. The thimble had little holes punched in its sides and thin ribbons of water were shooting out of the holes like see-through spaghetti. Honeysuckle's dragling, Pip, was fast asleep on a glossy green leaf far behind the bush, having grown tired of being drenched.

Rose, meanwhile, was heading back to the Fairythorn Tree with Pax, her dragling. To the Bigs, it looked like nothing more than a gnarly old tree, but the fairies knew better.

A Fairythorn Tree was a gateway through which Mother Nature's magic flowed into the Bigs' world. Not just magic, either. Every Fairythorn Tree had a tap which drew water straight from the springs of Fairyland – water so pure and magical that a single droplet quenched the thirst of the tallest tree for a month. And tonight, Rose was in charge of the tap!

Posy could see the fairy dust sparkling on Rose's beautiful, velvety-pink wings. They had only recently unfurled and Rose had discovered she was a Wish Fairy. She'd helped a little Big called Alice, who lived in the house at the end of the garden. Alice had wished for a friend and Rose had helped her to find one.

Posy twisted her neck to look at her own shoulders.

"Nothing!" she muttered. "Not a thing! Still grounded, like a caterpillar!"

Posy was desperate to fly. She glanced up at the circling Dash enviously. *If only I could work out what I'm good at,* she thought, *then my wings will sprout and I'll finally be able to take to the skies.*

Dash swooped down and licked her on the nose. Then he hopped into Posy's outstretched arms and snuggled up against her.

"I suppose I'm good at looking after you, Dash," she said. "But then we're good at looking after each other, aren't we? We're a team."

Dash stared up at her with his huge eyes and mewled like a newborn kitten with a sore throat.

"Love you, Dash," said Posy, burying her face in his warm, soft fur.

"Best friends for ever."

Dash soon started wriggling to get free again. Posy loosened her grip and off he flew. She turned her attention back towards the Fairythorn Tree. She giggled as she spotted Rose's dragling, Pax, splashing about in a muddy puddle under the tap that Rose was proudly guarding.

When a fairy gets her wings, her dragling changes to the same colour for ever, and so Pax had turned the same deep pink colour as Rose's wing-tips. Posy wasn't sure that Dash would be happy if he turned pink, and hoped that when she got her wings they'd be a colour Dash liked!

Posy watched as the Dewdrop Fairies queued by the Fairythorn tap, their crystal-clear wings almost invisible. In the daytime, any ray of light that hit them sent a rainbow of colours shooting off in all directions.

The fairies were waiting patiently to fill their acorn-shell buckets and other containers. One of the smaller fairies had the lid of a discarded toothpaste tube. Another was dragging a half-full yellow party balloon behind her.

Posy stretched and breathed in the cool, fresh air. It had been a long night, but her watch was almost over now. A few of the Choir Fairies had started to settle along the Fairythorn's branches. They were getting ready for the dawn chorus. It wouldn't be long until the sun came up and the day shift took over. Nothing could possibly go wrong before then. She would have bet her dragling on it.

Chapter 2

"Hello, Posy," said a fairy voice, making her jump. "How's your watch going?" Posy spun round to see a cuckoo, carrying Fleur, land gracefully on the roof behind her. Red flew down to join them as Fleur hopped off the bird's back. Dash zoomed towards his playmate and they rolled around together on the roof like a furry, green ball.

"Not a Grot Goblin in sight," said

Posy. She showed her friend the little golden horn. "Mother Nature told me to summon her with this if I see any."

At the words 'Grot Goblin', Red and Dash had jumped to attention and were now growling menacingly.

Fleur's green eyes widened with fear. Grot Goblins were the complete opposite of fairies.

While fairies were kind and good and did everything they could to help nature, Grot Goblins were masters of muck and did all they could to ruin gardens, destroy woodland and crush wildflower meadows. Nothing thrilled

a Grot Goblin more than a big pile of litter.

"But I thought Grot Goblins were never seen," said Fleur, nervously inching a little closer to her friend, as they settled down next to each other on the roof.

"They've been growing bolder,"

Posy explained. "A squirrel saw one yesterday, right by the Fairythorn Tree! He reported it to Mother Nature."

"What did it look like?" Fleur asked, then shuddered. "Not that I really want to know."

Posy shrugged. "Not sure," she admitted. "The squirrel hasn't said much since. Too scared apparently."

"I've heard that they're as tall as Bigs," said Fleur. "And they've got no eyelids, so they're always awake."

"I heard they have horrible stone teeth. All pointy and sharp," added Posy. "And they wear armour made from the Bigs' rubbish. But not the nice bits that we use to make things. You know – plastic bags, broken bottles, lumps of old chewing gum and stuff."

"Eww!" said Fleur.

"I know," said Posy. "Gross!"

As they looked out, something moved suddenly in the darkest part of the garden and Fleur and Posy grabbed each other in fright.

"It's okay," said Fleur, squinting. "It's just a hedgehog!" The two friends let out long sighs of relief.

Dash and Red were now marching around the shed roof like soldiers, their chests puffed out and their eyes serious. As well as being cute companions, draglings had a duty to protect their fairies.

"A really old fairy once told me that Grot Goblins can weave nightmares from spider's webs, and poke them into children's ears while they're sleeping," Fleur whispered.

"That's just stories for babies," said Posy, but she shivered all the same.

They stared at the giant webs that

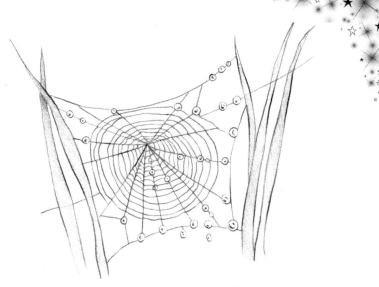

crisscrossed the garden, glittering in the grey light. The spiders had been busy all night, weaving the webs that would catch them their breakfast. "I bet you could make a fair few nightmares with that lot," said Fleur.

"And they're always hungry," said Posy. "Grot Goblins, I mean, not spiders."

There was a sudden burst of warm wind and Posy and Fleur scrambled to their feet. Mother Nature's face appeared in a swirl of twinkling mist before them. She had a habit of popping up when least expected, and in all sorts of magical ways. The last time Posy had seen her, Mother Nature had appeared as a talking cloud of fireflies!

"I need you to be brave, fairies," said her soft, friendly voice. "The Grot Goblins will only win if we let them."

Posy nodded enthusiastically. Mother Nature was right. They

couldn't let those horrible things bully them from their duties.

"Don't worry, Mother Nature," she said boldly, holding up the golden horn. "Grot Goblins don't bother me."

"That's the spirit, Posy," said the voice on the wind. "And remember, I am always at hand if you need me."

The wind died suddenly and the mist scattered. Mother Nature was gone, as quickly as she had appeared. Now it was all down to Posy!

Chapter 3

It was the moment just before dawn that things started to happen. Fleur had gone back to her watering work and Posy was doing a final circuit of the shed roof. The sky had lightened as the sun prepared to burst up over the horizon. Everything was calm and still… And then suddenly it wasn't any more.

Right in the middle of the garden, high in the air above the lawn, a doorway had appeared, like a big black rectangle cut out of the sky. It was the height of ten fairies, and had nothing behind it – just a gap where the world was supposed to be. Posy frowned and slowly made her way over to the edge of the roof to get a closer look.

"What is it?" she asked Dash, clutching her horn and peering into the garden. "It definitely wasn't there before. Where do you think it goes?"

Dash started to growl and paw at the roof tiles.

"What is it, boy?" asked Posy.

Posy realised she could hear a faint thudding noise, getting louder and louder, like hundreds of pairs of feet stomping towards them. Posy took a few steps back on the roof, but didn't dare take her eyes off the black doorway. All of a sudden the thudding stopped and there was silence again, except for Dash's low growling.

Posy wrapped her fingers around the golden horn. It was definitely time to call Mother Nature. But just as Posy brought the horn to her lips, a great blast of icy wind shot out of the strange doorway and bowled her right over. Dash scampered in front of her, his teeth bared in protection. Then, with a sudden shrieking, tornados exploded out through the doorway, one after another.

Posy watched in horror as the twisting tornados roared around the garden furiously. She saw flashes of troll-like beings in the murky whirlwinds. They were giving off a revolting stink, like a mixture of smelly feet and bin juice.

Posy wrinkled her nose. "You don't scare me," she shouted, even though her legs were wobbling with fear. She closed her eyes and blew the horn hard.

Nothing.

She blew it again, taking an even deeper breath this time. But it didn't make a sound.

"Oh no," said Posy, shaking it next to her ear. "It's not working!"

But somehow she had to

summon Mother Nature — she had to get help.

Posy ran to the edge of the roof and stared at the long drop to the ground. How she wished she had her wings. Any bird or creature that might have helped her off the roof had disappeared from the garden, well away from the shrieking whirlwinds, and she could hardly blame them.

Posy couldn't see any of the fairies who had been working in the area around the lawn, but she guessed they'd rushed to safety.

She glanced at Dash, who was

jumping and snapping at the gruesome tornados. There was nothing else for it. She'd have to jump.

Chapter 4

As Posy leapt off the shed roof, two magical things happened.

With a flash of light, Mother Nature's concerned face appeared in a cloud of swirling leaves, changing instantly to a soft cushioning hand when she spotted Posy. The hand scooped up the little fairy as she fell and gently deposited Posy on the edge of the lawn, away from the tornados, just as Dash crash-landed beside her. The golden horn had worked after all!

Posy lay on the grass, gasping, as Mother Nature made the second magical thing happen. She turned and smiled warmly at the horizon, at the spot where the sun was about to peek over, and Posy heard a loud whooshing. Suddenly the sun rocketed upwards into the air. It wasn't your average, lazy sunrise. This was instant day, like Mother Nature was flipping a switch!

As sunlight beamed across the garden and the shadows vanished, so did the Grot Goblins. Posy allowed herself a smile — she knew that Grot Goblins hated sunlight, like slugs hated salt. The filthy tornados shot into the centre of the garden and up through the black doorway. Then, air around the door wobbled, before the doorway disappeared completely and the garden went back to normal again.

Apart from the dirty smears on the lawn and the leaves that had been blasted around the garden, it was as if the goblins had never even been there.

"Well done, Posy," said the leafy face of Mother Nature, as the fairies emerged from their hiding places and gathered round. "You were very brave, as I knew you would be."

Posy felt like she was about to burst with pride. The golden horn glowed warmly against her chest. Posy looked down and saw it was shining like firelight.

"You can hang on to that," said Mother Nature, smiling, "just in case." But her smile faded as she looked at the damage done to the garden. "The Grot Goblins are gone for now," she began. "But they've done a lot of harm and it's up to us to fix it." She looked around at the fairies and nodded. "There's no time like the present, friends. To work!"

A cheer rang out around the garden.

Mother Nature smiled again and then was gone, leaving only a scattering of leaves on the grass where she had been.

For a moment no one moved or said anything. Then the Choir Fairies shook their wings, cleared their throats and began to sing the sunrise song. Soon, the birds didn't want to be outdone and joined in too. Even Boris, the ancient, warty toad from the pond, started croaking along to the melody. Posy sighed with relief. Mother Nature had arrived in the nick of time.

"Are you okay?" asked Rose, fluttering down beside Posy.

Posy nodded then hugged her friend. "I can't believe that just happened!"

A shadow passed over them as Honeysuckle and Fleur arrived by cuckoo. They hadn't got their wings yet either, so they relied on friendly garden creatures to give them lifts. Their draglings, Pip and Red, raced off into the long grass to play hide and seek with Dash and Pax.

"Nice jump," said Fleur, as Honeysuckle rushed straight over to give Posy a hug.

"I thought you were going to get splattered," she said in a small voice.

"Don't do that again."

"At least not until you've got wings," said Rose. "Or the use of something else's," she added, pointing towards the cuckoo taxi.

"Did the Grot Goblins do much damage?" Posy asked.

"Not too much," said Fleur. "Mother Nature got here before they had a chance to really wreck the place. The Bigs will probably think it was foxes. Could've been much worse, really." She frowned suddenly. "Unless you happen to be a spider," she added, pointing to the tattered remains of a cobweb above their heads.

Posy followed Fleur's gaze. The network of beautiful webs that the spiders had woven in the night was ruined, leaving just scraps and strands blowing in the breeze.

"Are they all like that?" Posy asked.

Honeysuckle nodded. "Afraid so. The Grot Goblins got every last one of them."

A red-bellied spider was dangling on a single silver thread from her wrecked web above. Spiders weren't the bravest of creatures, so Posy knew the spider would stay there until she was absolutely certain that the danger had passed. It was going to be a long and hungry day for her.

"The Grot Goblins were gathering up the webs," Honeysuckle explained. "I watched them do it. It was horrible."

Posy shivered. Had the old fairy been telling the truth about the Grot Goblins weaving nightmares?

"That's so mean," sighed Rose. Her big brown eyes filled up with tears. "The spiders worked really hard to make their webs and now they'll go hungry all day."

"Yes, but look," said Fleur, grinning suddenly. "The Web Fixer Fairies are coming."

About a hundred fairies with pointy, metallic wings were fluttering down onto the tattered webs. They were all wearing tiny white hard hats and goggles. Some of them were examining large cobweb drawings. Others were carrying sturdy-looking ropes of woven silk. The spiders raced eagerly back to their webs when they saw help had arrived. Rose sighed with relief.

"Of course! Thank bluebells for that," she said. "The fixers will sort everything out."

"Talking of fixing things," said Posy. "Shall we see what we can do to help clear up the garden?"

"Good idea," said Honeysuckle. Then she frowned. "Although last time Grot Goblins were here, I ended up mopping up a massive puddle of slime. It was—"

"Oi, fairies!" someone bellowed, interrupting Honeysuckle. "How long do I have to lie here being rudely ignored until one of you little flappers notices me?"

"Oh no!" said Fleur to the others, rolling her eyes. "Which one is it this time? Derek or Clive?"

Derek and Clive were the grumpiest pair of garden gnomes in the world. Fairy magic was not supposed to be used on humans, or on things humans made – like garden gnomes – but these two had been accidentally brought to life a year or so ago. Since then, Derek and Clive had done nothing but moan and cause misery for anyone unlucky enough to come across them.

"Come on," yelled the gnome, who was out of sight but certainly not out of earshot, "my head's next to a pile of fresh fox poo, and it flipping stinks!"

The fairies burst out laughing.

"Come on," grinned Posy. Her green eyes twinkled with mischief. "This is too good to miss."

Chapter 5

Posy, Honeysuckle and Fleur whizzed over to the garden pond on a cuckoo taxi. Rose followed, flapping her wings with more grace and control than she had managed on her early flights.

The Bigs who lived in the house kept changing their mind about where to put their garden gnomes. So Derek and Clive had a habit of popping up all over the place, much to the annoyance of the fairies. The most frequent spot was a weedy corner by the pond, surrounded by cracked flagstones.

As soon as they touched down, Posy could see that it was Clive who was in trouble. The two gnomes were almost identical, but Clive had a small crack in his pointy red hat. He was lying on his side with a thick blanket of cobwebs wrapped awkwardly around his chest and arms, like a half-finished Egyptian mummy.

Derek was on the other side of the pond, watching with mean delight as Clive lay dangerously near a very fresh-looking fox poo.

"Well don't just stand there gawping," snapped Clive. "Sprinkle me with fairy dust, or… or say abracadabra, or SOMETHING!"

"It doesn't work like that, Grumpy Pants," snapped Fleur. "And don't be so rude or we'll leave you right where you are. Fox whatsit and all."

"You wouldn't!" gulped Clive.

"We absolutely would," said Rose. "There are plenty of other things that need our help in the garden."

Clive sighed heavily then decided to keep quiet.

"One of those things sent him flying," shouted Derek. "He went down like a sack of spuds," he added, sniggering to himself.

"Oi! Who are you calling a sack of spuds?" demanded Clive. "If it came to a fight, we both know who'd win."

"That would be neither of you," said Posy, before Derek could reply. "You can't even move. How on Earth would you fight?"

"The day they can move around is the day I move out," muttered Fleur under her breath.

Rose knelt beside Clive and tugged at the cobwebs wrapped around his chest. "This stuff is pretty sturdy," she said. "Maybe we can use it to hoist him onto his… Er… Have you actually got feet, Clive?"

"Just get me up, Little Miss Flappy. And I'm made of concrete, I'll have you know. You'll need something stronger than cobwebs."

Fleur came over and dragged a long strand of cobweb away from

Clive, looping it around her shoulder like a length of rope.

"I'm going to take some of this stuff anyway," she said. "It'll easily carry a fairy's weight, and you never know when it will come in handy."

"Well it's not doing me any good," said Clive bluntly. "Just unwrap me and get me up!"

At that moment, Pip, Dash, Red and Pax came crashing through the long grass towards their fairies. Derek and Clive groaned loudly.

"Hasn't someone squished those fire-breathing nits yet?" yelled Derek.

The draglings started hopping across the lilypads on the pond in a very splashy game of tag.

"They're not bothering you," said Posy. "Let them play."

"All they ever do is bother us!" Clive protested. "It's their bloomin' hobby!"

Close behind the fallen gnome, a hydrangea bush began to rustle and shake. Everybody froze, except for Derek and Clive who were already permanently frozen. Out of the bush climbed a little girl with straight black hair that was tangled with stray leaves and twigs. She was eating a piece of toast and had a dollop of red jam on the front of her navy school uniform.

"It's Edie!" said Rose, beaming. "Which means Alice will be here any second."

Rose had found Edie as a friend for Alice when the little Big was lonely. Rose had asked the local burrowing animals to dig a tunnel between the girls' gardens. Then she had let herself be seen – very risky for fairies – in order to arrange their meeting.

Since that day, the two girls were always together. And sure enough, at that moment, Alice came dashing out of her back door, grinning as she ran across the lawn towards her friend.

Alice's dark hair was tied back in a messy ponytail, and she carried an empty jam jar and a goldfish net on a stick. The girls linked arms as they headed for the pond.

"Quick!" said Posy. "We can't be seen. Everyone hide!"

Chapter 6

Posy clung to the underside of a primrose leaf and held her breath. Rose ducked under a hedge, and Honeysuckle and Fleur hid in a tuft of long grass next to the pond. And although the gnomes were unable to hide, they had at least finally shut up. Only the draglings hadn't noticed Alice and Edie approaching.

"Dash," Posy cried out urgently. "Come here, boy!"

But Dash didn't hear. He was too busy splashing across the lilypads.

"DASH!" Posy yelled, "Red! Pip! Pax! HIDE!"

But none of the draglings were paying attention and Alice and Edie were almost at the pond. Posy opened her mouth to yell again, but instead of a shout, a funny little mewling sound came out of her mouth. Dash and his playmates froze at once and turned towards her in surprise. But it was too late. Alice and Edie had already reached the pond.

Alice frowned at the garden

gnome lying on his side. She laid her fishing gear on the grass and knelt down beside him.

"Poor you," she said. "Looks like a fox knocked you over." She brushed away the spiderwebs and placed him upright. "There you go," she said, then picked up her net.

"Remember, Mrs Lucas told us tadpoles spend most of their time eating algae close to the surface," said Edie. "Which sounds pretty disgusting to me."

"I'd much rather have pizza," agreed Alice.

"And ice cream for pudding," Edie nodded.

Posy peered out from under her primrose leaf and gasped. The draglings had finally noticed the Bigs and were huddled together on a lilypad.

"I think I can see something," Edie said. She crouched by the edge of the pond, leaning over so low that the ends of her hair just touched the water. "Have you got your net?"

Alice dipped the net into the water and dragged it along the surface. But all she'd caught was a great clump of mud.

"Yeuch!" she said, tipping it out with a heavy splash that bounced the draglings right off their lily pad. They fell into the water and got tangled up in some pondweed just as Alice plunged her net back into the pond.

"There's definitely something moving," she said, gliding the net over the surface carefully. "Right… here…" Her tongue was sticking out with concentration. "Got it!" she announced, lifting the net out of the pond triumphantly. "Pass me the jar please, Edie. This will mean extra marks from Mrs Lucas for sure!"

Edie held out the jar and Alice slopped the contents of her net into it. Posy's heart sank as she peered into the pond. She couldn't see the draglings any more, so that must mean the worst… they were in the jar.

The girls waved a quick 'see you'

to each other, with Alice heading back inside with the jar to finish getting ready for school and Edie scrambling back into the tunnel.

Frozen with shock, Posy could do nothing. The other fairies came out of hiding, white and shaken. Rose was crying, Honeysuckle had gone as pale as daisy petals, and Fleur was stomping around furiously. Posy felt like someone had just chopped off one of her arms. Dash had always been by her side. Now she felt a gaping, dragling-shaped hole in her heart.

"What are we going to do?" said

Honeysuckle in a panicky whimper.

"Celebrate?" suggested Derek.

"Nice one," cackled Clive.

"Don't you dare," snapped Fleur. "Or I'll get a badger to tip you both over and do its business on you!"

That shut them up.

"Where do you think Alice is taking them?" asked Rose in a shaky voice. "And why?"

"It's got something to do with Mrs Lucas," said Posy. "I heard them talking about it. She must be another Big, who wanted them to collect tadpoles." She stared at the house.

The kitchen window was open. "Come on," she said, beckoning to the others, "we need to get inside."

Five flaps of a plump wood pigeon's wings got them to the Bigs' house. Even Rose had hopped on the bird. She was feeling too upset to fly straight.

They landed right on the windowsill and crept through the open window onto a shelf behind the sink. Luckily there was a handy flowerpot of violets to hide behind.

"Budge up," said Fleur, nudging Honeysuckle. "I can't see anything."

Posy stuck her head up and parted the violets to scan the room. The radio was on. Alice was sitting at a small, round table, drinking apple juice and munching cornflakes. She'd placed the jar right in front of her on the table. Alice's mum, Mrs Miller, was packing Alice's lunchbox for school. Mr Miller was burning a slice of toast. He pulled a face when he joined Alice at the table and saw the jar. "Do we have to look at that while we're eating, Alice?"

"It's my homework, Dad," she protested. "Tadpoles. I'm taking them to school this morning. We're doing the life cycle of the frog. I told Mrs Lucas we had a pond and she asked me to catch some tadpoles and bring them in," she explained.

"Well, it's putting me off my breakfast," sniffed Mr Miller. He got to his feet, picked up the jar and moved it to the kitchen windowsill. Then he sat back down again with a heavy thump.

The jar was just centimetres away from the fairies now and they gasped at the sight of their draglings paddling furiously on the water's surface, surrounded by pondweed.

"Red!" called Fleur, cupping her hands around her mouth. She was halfway round the flowerpot before Rose could stop her.

"Don't," hissed Rose. "The Bigs will see you."

"I don't care," Fleur replied. "I just want my dragling back."

"We all want our draglings back, Fleur," pleaded Posy, "but you know we can't just let the Bigs see us."

"But Alice has already seen us. Well, she's seen Rose, anyway," Fleur argued. "And Pax too."

"Yes, but Alice is only a little Big,"

said Rose. "They're okay. It's the big Bigs you've got to worry about." She nodded over at Alice's parents. "And there are two of them right there."

Fleur stamped her feet, her green eyes filling with tears.

"But how are we going to rescue the draglings?" she demanded.

"They can't swim about in there for ever," Honeysuckle added. "Pip hasn't even had her breakfast yet. She gets properly grumpy when she's hungry."

Posy gazed at the jar, longingly. It was hopeless. Dash was right there,

almost within arm's length, but he might as well have been on another planet. *Oh Dash,* she thought to herself, *why did you have to go and get yourself caught?*

At that moment, Dash turned

and paddled over to the side of the jar, and stared right into Posy's eyes. Her head filled with words so loud she felt even the Bigs would hear them.

We didn't see the net coming, said the voice in her head. *Please save us! The tadpoles are being horrid.*

Posy's mouth dropped open and she quickly grabbed Rose.

"Did you hear that?" she spluttered. "The thing about the tadpoles being horrid?"

Rose looked confused. "What are you talking about?" she asked.

Posy looked back at Dash, who

was still staring straight at her. "I just spoke to Dash in my thoughts," she said, "and I think he spoke back to me. Is that mad?"

Rose frowned. "A bit, yes. Are you feeling all right?"

Posy remembered the funny mewling sound she'd made when she tried to warn the draglings and began to wonder if the two things were linked. But there was no time to worry about that now. The other weed-covered draglings had joined Dash by the glass and were going nuts at the sight of their fairies.

Pip and Pax were headbutting the side of the jar. Red and Dash were trying to get out by burning a hole in the jar's metal lid.

"If the Bigs look now they'll soon realise those aren't tadpoles!" gasped Honeysuckle. "We need to move fast. What should we do?"

Without a word, Posy stared at the draglings sternly and held a finger to her lips.

Be still and quiet, she thought, *or the Bigs will spot you and take you from us for ever.*

The draglings stopped their

bashing and burning at once and Posy felt a tingling sensation on her shoulder blades, right where her wings would be.

Fleur looked suspiciously from Posy to the draglings, then back to Posy.

"Did you just do something?" she asked.

"I'm not sure," Posy replied honestly. "But if I did, it worked."

The draglings were treading water calmly.

"What next, then?" asked Fleur.

They watched as Alice slurped

up the milk from the bottom of her cereal bowl.

Posy shrugged. "We go where Alice goes, I suppose."

The little Big jumped up and brought her bowl and glass to the sink. She grabbed the jar from the windowsill and held it up to the light. Luckily there was too much pond weed in there for her to see much.

"Have you got the rest of your homework, Alice?" asked her mum.

Alice clapped a hand to her mouth. "Hang on, I left my book upstairs."

Her mum tutted. "Hurry up, or

you'll be late for school."

Alice put the jar down next to her school bag, on the worktop opposite the windowsill, then dashed into the hall. The fairies could hear her thundering up the stairs and across the landing in the direction of her bedroom.

"We have to get into Alice's bag!" said Rose.

"But we'll never make it over there without being seen," said Honeysuckle.

"We have to do something," Rose replied. "Once Alice takes them away we won't know where they are any more." Her eyes filled with tears as she looked at the draglings and the gigantic distance that separated them. "And then what would we do?"

Chapter 7

"I've got a plan!" said Posy, clicking her fingers. "Fleur, have you got that cobweb rope?"

Fleur hoisted the rope off her shoulder and tossed it to Posy. "Knew it would come in handy," she said, smiling, as Posy tested it for stretchiness.

"Perfect," said Posy. She tied one end around a violet stalk and handed the other to Rose. "Do you think you can fly over there and tie this to something?" she said seriously.

Rose looked over at Alice's mum, nervously. She was pottering about all over the place, tidying things up and cleaning with a pink duster. Mr Miller was still sitting at the table reading the back of the cornflakes packet.

"I think so," she said at last, looking from fairy to fairy. "I guess it's our only chance if we want to get our draglings back."

"Okay," said Fleur. "Let's get on with it."

It was all systems go once Alice's

mum had left the kitchen to put the bins out.

"Now, Rose!" said Honeysuckle.

Rose launched herself from the side of the flowerpot and fluttered away, clutching the end of the rope. A trail of fairy dust sparkled in the air behind her. She flew quickly across the room to the worktop opposite the windowsill, and tied the rope around

the wooden branch of a mug tree.

"Come on," she said, beckoning to others frantically. "Hurry!"

Fleur went first, then Posy, then Honeysuckle. They ran across the strand of spider's thread like the world's fastest tightrope walkers, their arms outstretched for balance.

It was all going to plan until

Mr Miller scraped his chair back and stood up with his empty plate, turning towards the sink. The fairies were only a carrot's length away from him.

"Now what?" hissed Fleur over her shoulder.

"Hide?" suggested Posy, in Fleur's ear.

"Hide where?" asked Fleur. "We're on a spiderweb rope in the middle of thin air."

"Just keep still!" Honeysuckle called from the back of the line.

The three of them crouched low and froze. They watched nervously as Mr Miller rinsed his plate under the tap, whistling tunelessly to himself. He was so close to the spider thread that every movement he made, the rope swayed dangerously. The fairies clung on tightly.

Mr Miller stacked his plate on the drainer, missing the tiny strand of rope by millimetres. Then he marched out of the room, with no idea how near he'd come to fairies.

"Phew, that was close," said Posy as she got to her feet. "Come on."

They raced across to the worktop where Rose was waiting, hidden behind the mug tree. The four fairies dashed to the jar to see their draglings.

Honeysuckle stroked the glass between her and the paddling Pip. "Poor Pip," she said. "I think she's lost weight already."

Just then, Alice came thumping back down the stairs from her bedroom, clutching her exercise book.

"Come on," said Posy. "Alice is ready to go. Everyone into the bag."

Chapter 8

"I feel sick," groaned Honeysuckle.

The fairies were sitting at the bottom of Alice's swinging school bag, trying not to get squashed by the books, pencils, water bottle and apple that were inside. Alice liked to skip, rather than walk, so things were rolling about all over the place, the fairies included.

"It can't be too much further," said Rose hopefully, tucking her wings in to protect them. "She's been skipping along for ages."

They stopped sharply and the zip above their heads was suddenly ripped open. Sunlight poured in, followed by Alice's rummaging hand.

"Mum! Where's that friendship bracelet I made for Edie?" said Alice, as the fairies dived about like acrobats to avoid her searching fingers. "I must have left it at home."

"We haven't got time to go back for it now," said Mrs Miller. "You'll have to give it to her after school."

Alice rummaged harder.

"Ouch!" squeaked Fleur, as she bashed into the water bottle.

"But that's ages away," moaned Alice to her mum.

Her hand appeared again near the zip, and then the bag lurched to one side as Alice shook it. The fairies tumbled to one end, and Posy squealed as the apple began rolling towards them like a huge green boulder.

"We're going to be flattened by fruit!" said Fleur.

"This way!" said Honeysuckle, climbing over the pencils and into a dark corner.

Led by Fleur, the other three fairies clambered over the pencils too, safe from the apple at last. But Honeysuckle was nowhere to be seen.

"Honeysuckle...?" Fleur called, confused. She stepped into the dark corner too, Rose and Posy close behind.

Suddenly there was light, and Fleur realised what had happened. They had fallen through a hole in the corner of Alice's bag! She quickly copied Honeysuckle, who had grabbed hold of a loose thread at the worn edges on the hole.

"Quick, Rose, Posy, hold on tight!" she cried in warning.

All four friends dangled precariously as Alice continued skipping, oblivious to their plight.

"Well that didn't go quite to plan," said Honeysuckle.

"Now what?" squeaked Posy. "I don't know about you, but I can't hang on like this for much longer."

"My hands keep slipping," Rose wailed.

"Mine too!" yelled Fleur.

"I think we're almost there," Posy called to the others as Alice seemed to slow down. "Hold on!"

Honeysuckle and Rose nodded

miserably. But then the bag jolted violently as Alice jumped to avoid a puddle, and the fairies slapped together like dominoes. They yelped as, one by one, they fell to the ground with a thud.

"So much for hanging on!" grumbled Honeysuckle.

The fairies brushed themselves down as they watched Alice and the jar of draglings skip away into the distance.

There were Bigs everywhere, travelling to work and school, walking their dogs, nipping to the shops for milk and newspapers. Their huge feet and the screeches of wheels from scooters, buggies, bikes and buses were deafening. Honeysuckle looked like she might cry.

"I miss Pip," she sniffed.

None of them had ever been so far away from the Fairythorn Tree before, and they didn't even have their draglings for protection. They were lost and alone in the Bigs' gigantic world.

Chapter 9

"Hello, fairies. Need a lift?"

Posy and her friends looked up to see a ginger tomcat padding up to them. His paws were white and he had a very pink nose.

"Mother Nature had a word," he purred. "Said you might need a little help. A gentle push in the right direction." He sat down next to them and lazily cleaned his ears.

"Oh, yes please," Honeysuckle

said eagerly. "Thank you, cat."

Posy grinned and clambered onto the cat's soft, warm back, motioning for her friends to join her.

It looked like their luck might be turning.

The fairies held on tight to the tomcat's fur as he carried them all the way to the gates of the school playground. They slid off quickly and thanked the cat, and he turned for home to take his morning nap.

Lessons had already started, so the playground was empty except for the four tiny fairies. They stood in the middle of the vast space, staring up at the school building. It looked very, very big.

"Our draglings are in there somewhere," said Posy, squeezing her fists in determination. "Let's find them and get us all home."

"But where do we start?" said Rose.

"With the right transport," said Fleur. She pointed at a squirrel bounding over the school fence. "And he looks perfect."

Soon the squirrel was hopping from

windowsill to windowsill while the fairies peered into every classroom in turn.

"Is that Alice?" Honeysuckle asked.

"No, that girl's way older, and she's got blonde hair!" said Fleur.

"Stop asking every five seconds and try looking for a girl who actually looks like Alice, will you?"

"How can you tell, when they're sitting down all hunched over like that?" Honeysuckle sighed. "Bigs all look the same to me."

"Oh, this is hopeless," said Posy. "We've been searching for ever."

"There are still a few classrooms left," said Rose. "Don't give up."

But Alice wasn't in the next three classrooms, either. Or in the assembly hall. Or out playing rounders on the school field.

Soon, they had reached the final classroom, at the end of the block. Posy almost didn't dare look in, she was so worried that Alice wouldn't be inside. But when Fleur nudged her and started bouncing up and down on the squirrel's back, she quickly took a peek.

There she was! Alice was sitting around a table with five other children, including Edie. Their teacher was a woman with bright red hair and thick black-framed glasses. She was talking to the children about whizzy words and making a list on the board behind her. Posy looked further into the classroom and spotted the jam jar on a desk at the far side of the room. A shiny new fish tank sat next to it, completely empty.

"I guess they're supposed to go in that," said Fleur.

"Lucky for us they haven't put them in yet," said Posy. "Or the Bigs would definitely have found out what's really in that jar."

Honeysuckle slid off the squirrel's back and pressed her nose to the glass window.

"How do we get in?" she asked.

"I can help you with that," a very small voice said. It was so small the fairies weren't sure they'd heard anything at all.

"Oi," it said, a little louder this time, "do you want my help or not?"

Rose swung her head round. "Who said that?"

"Down here," said the voice.

The fairies looked to the ground, where a little grey mouse was sitting up on its hind legs.

"I know a way in," said the mouse. "As long as you don't mind getting a bit dirty."

The fairies grinned from ear to ear. They didn't mind at all, not if it meant getting their draglings back.

The squirrel took the fairies down to the ground and then the little grey mouse led them to a hole in the school wall.

"Through here," she said. "It's a bit dark, but just keep going."

The fairies crawled in behind the mouse and made their way along a narrow, dusty tunnel. It was so dark that Posy couldn't see her hand in front of her face. But when Rose gave a flutter of her wings, the shower of fairy dust that sparkled off them was bright enough to light up the gloom.

Soon enough, they popped up through a hole that the mouse had gnawed in the skirting board. Posy couldn't believe it. They'd made it. She stared up at the jam jar and words filled her head again. This time she was certain it was Dash.

You came to rescue us, like you promised, he said. *Thank you!*

Chapter 10

Their goal was in sight, but the fairies had no idea what to do next.

"We can't stay here," said Fleur. They were still standing next to the mouse hole at the edge of the classroom. "We'll be seen and scooped into the tank with our draglings!"

"I say we hide for now," said Posy. "Wait until the coast is clear."

The classroom was cluttered with school equipment, so it wasn't hard to find a hiding place. They climbed up a chair leg and into a pot of pencils on a small table and gazed out at the colourful walls of the classroom.

There were displays about dinosaurs, the Tudors, the Ancient Egyptians and the moon landings. A huge model of the planets hung from the ceiling, next to a cardboard rocket. There were shelves crammed with books, and a blue reading tent in one corner. The fairies thought it all looked lovely.

They'd only been in the pot for a few minutes when the bell rang for break-time and Alice and her friends rushed out into the playground. The fairies looked at each other, hoping this would be their chance to free the draglings, but their hearts sank when the teacher stayed in the classroom and began marking exercise books.

The fairies waited patiently until lunchtime – by now they were all sitting cross-legged on the floor of the pencil pot. But when the bell rang and they jumped up, disappointment flooded through them as another teacher arrived to run a French club.

By two o'clock, Honeysuckle and Rose were fast asleep, Fleur was chewing her nails nervously and Posy was twisting loose staples into a little pointy crown.

"This is ridiculous," said Posy. "We're going to be here for ever!"

"We'll have to get the classroom to ourselves at some point," said Fleur. Her eyes suddenly widened. "Watch out," she said. "Little Big alert!"

A lanky boy with sandy blonde hair was lolloping in their direction.

Posy nudged Rose and Honeysuckle awake. The boy was heading straight for them and there was no time to hide.

"Oh no!" said Fleur, as the fairy friends huddled together.

The little boy reached out and wrapped his hand around the pot of pencils. He glanced

down, and for a moment he just stared, blankly. Then he blinked and rubbed his eyes. Four tiny fairies stared back at him.

"Any time today would be good, please, Jamie," the teacher sighed. "Three different coloured pencils. Any colours. You can choose."

Jamie looked at the teacher, then back down at the fairies.

"Are you all right?" asked the teacher. "You've gone quite pale. You look like you've seen a ghost."

Jamie shook his head, then nodded, then shook his head again.

"Not a ghost, Miss," he said. "Fairies!"

"Oh no," groaned Fleur. "Busted!"

The teacher rolled her eyes. "I haven't got time for your nonsense, Jamie," she said. "Save it for when we're writing stories. Three pencils. Now, please!"

"But, Miss," Jamie protested. "There's fairies in the pencil pot!" He frowned. "At least, I think they're fairies. Only one of them has wings. Do all fairies have wings?"

Jamie's classmates burst out laughing.

"Fairies!" another boy teased. "Been playing with your sister's dollies again, Jamie?"

But among the laughing faces, Alice and Edie were suddenly sitting up very straight in their seats. They knew all about fairies. They knew there was a chance that Jamie was telling the truth.

"That's enough, Jamie," the teacher said sternly. "I won't ask you again."

Jamie opened his mouth to argue, but shut it again when he saw his teacher's face. Instead he took three pencils out of the pot and placed it back, fairies and all, on the table where he'd found it.

He gave the pot a tiny wave as he turned for his desk. Honeysuckle and Rose waved back. Fleur stuck her tongue out.

"Phew, that was close," said Posy. "Thank goodness grown-up Bigs don't believe in fairies."

"That little Big won't be so sure now, at least for a few years to come," giggled Honeysuckle.

"But what do we do now?" said Fleur. "We're getting nowhere fast.

I thought rescue missions were meant to be exciting."

"Be patient," said Rose, settling back down among the pencils. "We can't let ourselves get caught by the Bigs. I'm going to have a nap while we wait."

She closed her eyes and leaned back against the smooth wood. "Wake me up when something happens."

Chapter 11

It wasn't until home time that the fairies could finally make their move.

"Thank sunbeams for that!" said Fleur as the final bell rang. "It's getting really hot in this pencil pot."

Rose stretched and rubbed her eyes. "I thought it was quite comfortable," she yawned.

"We'll move the tadpoles to the tank tomorrow," said the teacher to Alice's class as they scuttled through the door. "Thanks again for bringing them in, Alice."

"Hooray!" said Honeysuckle. "Now, go home, teacher Big!"

"Uh-oh," said Posy, peering out through the pencils.

Alice and Edie were making their way across the classroom with Jamie. He was pointing at the pencil pot with the same confused look on his face from earlier.

"Trouble at twelve o'clock," said Posy.

"But it's quarter past three," said Fleur, looking at the clock on the wall.

Posy rolled her eyes.

"Just hide!" she snapped. "The Bigs are coming."

The fairies ducked down obediently.

"Are you sure this isn't a joke, Jamie?" Edie was saying.

Posy held her breath and squeezed her eyes tight shut. They were about to be discovered.

"It's really not," said Jamie. "You wait and see. I—"

"Jamie, Edie and Alice," the teacher called out. "Would you come over here for a moment, please?

I want you three to be in charge of moving the tadpoles tomorrow."

"Awesome!" said Jamie, as the three of them headed away.

"Phew!" said Posy. "That was close. Do you think they've gone for good?"

"I'll take a look," said Fleur.

"Be careful," said Rose, as Fleur clambered to her feet and peeked over the edge of the pencil pot.

"The teacher Big's talking to them over by the jar," she reported back, "but Alice keeps looking this way. She's definitely on to us."

Posy jumped up to join Fleur and pointed to the reading tent nearby.

"That's only a couple of bunny hops away," she said. "If we run really fast we might be able to make it without being seen."

"Might?" said Rose from the bottom of the jar. "We have to be sure!"

"We don't really have a choice," said Fleur. "I know we'll have no cover until we get to the tent. But as we're about to be discovered anyway, I say we go for it." She looked out at the Bigs again anxiously. "But let's do it quickly, before I change my mind."

Rose nodded, realising Fleur was right, and flew over to the tent with no trouble at all. The rest of the fairies, though, had to clamber out of the pencil pot and shimmy down a table leg to the floor.

"I'd eat a bucket of dragling dung for a pair of wings right now," said Posy, as she hung over the edge of the table.

"I'd kiss a grot goblin," said Fleur, as she clung to the leg and slid down, eyes closed.

As soon as she reached the floor, Fleur scampered over to the reading tent and vanished through the flaps. Posy was next. She could hear Honeysuckle running behind her but she didn't dare look back. Her heart was thumping. It was all too easy to imagine a Big spotting them and a giant hand snatching her up into the air.

At last, Posy tumbled down to safety through the dark-blue folds of tent fabric,

followed immediately by Honeysuckle.

The fairies looked around. It was nice inside the reading tent – warm and dark with cushions scattered around the edges, and a ceiling covered in glowing, star-shaped stickers. "I wish we'd hidden in here instead of that stupid pencil pot," said Fleur. She settled down on a faded red velvet cushion and sighed. "Much squidgier than pencils."

At the sound of footsteps, Fleur sprang to her feet again.

"Come on then, Jamie," came Edie's voice. "Show us the fairies."

"I saw them in that pot, I promise," Jamie insisted. "Four of them. Well, at least one fairy — maybe the others were elves. They didn't have wings."

"Elves?" Posy huffed. "We look nothing like elves!"

The fairies went quiet as they heard the pencils shaken about in their pot.

"Well there's nothing here now except pencils," said Alice.

Edie sighed. "And I almost believed you, Jamie," she said, sounding disappointed. "Nice try."

"But I did see them," Jamie

moaned. "I swear on my skateboard! And anyway, look at that sparkly stuff. That's evidence, that is. That's fairy dust! I'm not making that up, am I?"

"Oh dear," said Rose, clapping a hand over her mouth. "That must be my wings. I can't help sprinkling fairy dust. I'm sorry!"

"It does look a lot like fairy dust," said Edie.

"You mean you've seen it before?" said Jamie. "Have you seen actual fairies, then? Are there more of them?"

At the other end of the classroom, someone clapped their hands.

"Come on, you three," said the teacher. "That pencil pot's had enough attention for one day. Scoot."

The fairies held their breath as they listened to the little Bigs leave, then the sound of the teacher Big scooping up her papers and packing them into her bag. Finally, the classroom lights flicked off and the door banged shut.

"At last!" said Fleur, her eyes gleaming like emeralds. "Let's go and get our draglings."

Chapter 12

Rose stuck her head out of the tent and into the empty classroom. "The coast is clear, I think. It's hard to tell in the dark."

"I'll settle for the dark," said Posy. "It's perfect for an undercover rescue."

"Why don't you fly over and let the draglings out, Rose," suggested Fleur. "It'll be quicker."

"Good idea," said Rose. "You stay

here and keep watch, in case a Big comes back." She bent her knees ready to take off.

"Hold on," said Posy. She reached up and removed a thorn from her headdress.

"Here, take this," she said, handing it to Rose. "It might be useful."

"Good thinking, Posy," Rose smiled.

She took off and, with a spray of sparkles, looped the loop and soared towards the jar.

Posy, Honeysuckle and Fleur waited impatiently by the tent.

"Where is she?" said Posy, peering across the classroom. "I can't see any of her fairy dust. Do you think she's let the draglings out yet?"

"I hope so," said Honeysuckle. "They've been treading water all day. They must be exhausted."

Suddenly, words began to fill Posy's head and she grinned. She was getting used to it now.

Rose is here, said Dash. *She's sawing through the lid with a sharp pointy thing! But the tadpoles are cross because she woke them up.*

Sit tight, Posy replied, in her head.

You're almost free.

Rose is trying to peel the lid back, said Dash. *But it's too heavy... Wait, Pax and Red are helping... Yes! We're out!*

The familiar sound of little growly catlike mewls rang around the classroom. The draglings were free!

"It's them!" cried Honeysuckle.

"Dash!" shouted Posy, out loud this time. "I'm here! Come here, boy!"

The four draglings, followed by Rose, flew across the room, and Posy grinned as Dash mewled with excitement and puffed out a little green fireball. She held out her arms and, without thinking, she mewled back. Fleur looked at her in astonishment.

"Did you just mewl?" she asked.

Posy blushed. "Erm… yes," she said quietly. "Although, I'm not sure why."

Dash, dripping with pond water from the tadpole jar, was licking Posy's face excitedly. His soaking fur ponged, but Posy didn't care. All that mattered was that they were back together. She had felt so lonely without him. Dash stopped wriggling for a moment and stared at her with his massive eyes.

I knew you'd come, he said in Posy's head.

I promised didn't I? Posy thought back. *Best friends for ever.*

The fairies and their draglings found their way out of the school the same way the fairies had come in – by mouse tunnel.

Posy crawled behind Rose along

the dark, narrow passageway. She tried not to think about her itching shoulder blades – it was so bad, she wanted to stop and rub her back against the low ceiling of the tunnel.

Something's definitely happening to me, she thought to herself, crossing her fingers. *Please, please let it be what I think it is.*

The sun had almost set by the time the fairies and their draglings emerged into the playground. They looked up to see birds flying back to their favourite trees to roost for the night.

Posy felt a sudden rush of warmth from the top of her head to the tips of her toes.

"Rose?" she asked, nervously, "what did it feel like when you got your wings?"

"Like May Day had come early," said Rose, brushing tunnel dirt from her knees. "Although it tingled a bit, I can tell you. Wait, have you—"

But before a wide-eyed Rose could finish, she was interrupted by the tinkling sound of a thousand tiny bells…

Chapter 13

For Posy, it all happened so quickly. One moment, nothing. The next... wings!
Posy's wings were truly beautiful. They were rich purple, trimmed with snow-white borders, and they fanned out like peacock

feathers, sprinkling fairy dust on everyone.

For a second, Posy stood in shocked silence. Then she burst out laughing and tried to twist round to see them properly.

"They're gorgeous," cooed Honeysuckle.

"They suit you," grinned Fleur.

Posy flapped her new wings together and more fairy dust puffed off them, like powdered sugar on a jam doughnut. She looked up at Dash, circling proudly above. He had turned a lovely shade of purple, with bright green trimmings, although it was hard to tell the difference between the new markings and the pond sludge that clung to his tail.

As the fairies admired Posy and Dash, a sudden gust of wind came from nowhere, accompanied by a shower of apple-blossom petals.

"Fairies, look!" said Fleur, standing to attention.

Mother Nature's face appeared in the swirling petals.

"Hello, fairies," she began. "Well done for rescuing your draglings. Once again you were all very brave."

She turned to the draglings and her face grew stern. "You draglings need to learn to behave," she scolded. "You must always stay close to your fairies and listen to them when they call you. Otherwise, you might get yourselves into even worse trouble next time."

I hope you're listening, Posy said to Dash in her head.

"I don't want to think about what would have happened if the Bigs had found you," Mother Nature continued. "You're very lucky to have such brave fairies on your side."

The draglings bowed their heads in shame.

Mother Nature continued ticking off the draglings as the fairies watched, before she finally announced, "I think you've learned your lesson now. We'll say no more about it."

She smiled warmly again. "Congratulations on your new wings, Posy."

"Thank you, Mother Nature," said Posy, curtseying. Then she frowned. "Though I'm not entirely sure what I got them for."

"Haven't you wondered how you

can speak to Dash all of a sudden?" Mother Nature asked, the breeze still blowing around her. "Or communicate with the other draglings, for that matter?"

"You can speak dragling?" asked Fleur, staring at Posy. "It all makes sense now!"

Posy shrugged. "I wasn't sure what I was hearing at first," she admitted. "To be honest, I thought I might be going a bit mad."

"Dear me, no," Mother Nature chuckled. "You're a Dragling Fairy, Posy. You've been given the gift of dragling language so you can train the young ones. Rather an important job, I'd say, given what happened today." She eyed the draglings with a half smile.

"But let's not forget the old draglings," Mother Nature continued. "They're full of wisdom and good advice. They can tell you all sorts, from how to use fairy fire correctly, to basic tree training."

Posy noticed her wings were glowing in the gathering dusk. She had never felt so happy.

"Thank you, Mother Nature,"

she said. "I'll be the best Dragling Fairy that ever lived."

"I'm sure you will, Posy. Goodbye, fairies. I hope you enjoy the sunset. I'm planning something spectacular for this evening. Oh, and I've arranged a lift for you. It'll be here soon to carry you home."

The wind died down as suddenly as it had picked up, and the petals of Mother's Nature's face tumbled to the floor as she disappeared.

"Well go on then, Posy," said Rose, wiggling her own wings. "Aren't you going to try them out?"

"It's not like you really wanted them or anything," teased Fleur.

"You're right!" said Posy. "What on earth am I doing down here?"

She bent at the knees, took a deep breath and soared into the early evening sky.

Posy's flying was a bit wonky at first, but by her third lap of the playground, she'd completely got the hang of it.

When she made a particularly graceful landing, finishing with her arms aloft, her friends gave her a round of applause.

"How was it?" asked Fleur eagerly.

Posy winked. "Even better than I dreamed it would be!"

Just as Posy was preparing to take off again, their lift arrived — an owl, with very long legs, nut-brown feathers and a pale, heart-shaped face.

"Good evening, young fairies," hooted the owl. "Who's heading for the Fairythorn Tree?"

"I could fly…" said Rose, "but I am quite tired. Yes please, owl."

"Me too, please," Honeysuckle said, climbing onto the owl's back.

"And me," said Fleur. "Thanks!"

"Don't mention it," said the owl. He turned to Posy and asked, "You, miss?"

"No, thank you," said Posy, grinning. "I think I'll fly myself home tonight."

The sunset was as spectacular as Mother Nature had said it would be.

Posy followed the owl, with the draglings tumbling along behind. She grinned as the sky exploded into shades of orange and red and the world below was lost in shadow.

As they flew, they could hear the Choir Fairies joining the birds in their evening chorus. The beautiful voices rolled over the treetops, leading Posy and her friends home.

Chapter 14

Posy tied the friendship bracelet around Dash's ankle. She had one too, on her wrist. She'd made them by dying tiny strands of spider-silk with blackberry paste and plaiting the purple strands together.

They were both sitting on the hammock in her bedroom, which she'd decorated simply. There was a fluffy rug made from woven dandelion clocks on the floor, a cotton-reel bedside table

and a large round bottle-top mirror that was draped with Posy's collection of feathered headdresses. They had been back at the Fairythorn Tree for a few hours and the moon was now high in the sky.

Posy sat back on her heels to admire her work.

"There we go," she said. She held up her wrist and grinned. "Friendship bracelets, just like the little Bigs have. Now we're even more matching."

There was a knock on the door and Rose burst in.

"I've come to get you," she panted urgently, Pax rushing in behind her.

"It's not the Grot Goblins again, is it?" asked Posy.

She reached for the golden horn lying on her bedside table.

Rose shuddered. "No, thank goodness. It's something much nicer than that."

Posy swung her feet over the side of the hammock.

"Have Derek and Clive been thrown out with the rubbish?" she asked hopefully.

Rose grinned. "Even better. Come with me."

Rose skipped towards the tunnel opening that led to Edie's garden, and into the big, cosy alcove just beneath the hydrangea bush. There, with a note tied to its chimney, was a beautiful, handmade fairy house.

Rose hovered like a humming bird while Posy read the note aloud.

Hello fairies,

We hope you like your fairy house. It took us all of Saturday to make. We'll add more furniture and stuff when we work out how to stop the legs falling off things. Thank you again for the tunnel, which is totally cool!

By the way, were you at our school today? We think you were. We hope you liked it. Did you see the tadpoles that we caught in the garden pond? There are seven altogether!

Hope to see you soon.

Alice and Edie xxx

The fairy house had a sign saying 'NO BOYS ALLOWED' with a skull and crossbones hanging over its door. It was made from a shoebox, decorated mostly with garden treasures – dried grass, sticks, bark and acorns – but there were also some multi-coloured necklace beads and

a few pink feathers that Posy recognised from Mrs Miller's duster. There was a neat little pebble pathway running up to the doorway, which was cut into the shoebox.

The fairies peeked inside. The walls were papered with actual wallpaper! And there was a patch of dark green carpet glued on the floor, with four pincushion bean bags for Posy and her friends to curl up in.

"We should leave them some wildflowers as a thank-you present," said Rose, settling into one of the beanbags.

"Good idea," said Posy, grinning. "It's not every day you get a house like this built for you!"

The next day, and for many days that followed, Dash and the other draglings were much better behaved. They didn't stray far from their fairies, and they listened carefully to every warning or instruction. None of them wanted to end up in a jam jar of dirty pond water again.

They even left Derek and Clive alone, although without anything to complain about, Posy wondered if the gnomes secretly missed the draglings.

Posy loved her new job as a Dragling Fairy, and Dash, Red, Pax and Pip were part of her very first young dragling's class. She'd taken Mother Nature's advice and spoken to the wise old draglings. They had given her lots of good tips.

"Right then you lot," Posy mewled firmly, "pay attention at the back!"

It was late afternoon, the sun was high in the sky, and Posy was standing in the shade of the Fairythorn Tree. A crowd of young draglings sat in front of her trying very hard to behave. They were surrounded by a few curious fairies – including Honeysuckle, Rose and Fleur. Posy put her hands on her hips like she meant business.

"Lesson number one," she began, her green eyes sparkling with mischief. "How not to get caught by the Bigs."

Rose

Rose is kind, sensitive and gentle. She's always trying to make things better for those around her, but is also a worrier. She likes sparkly things, flower petals and weaving decorations into her hair.

Posy

Posy is unstoppable and brave. She adores animals and is often found riding butterflies or chatting to squirrels. Posy loves to wear feathers and her clothes are mainly assembled from things she finds in nature.

Honeysuckle

Honeysuckle is a dreamer. She's a bit dizzy and clumsy, but very sweet with it. She has boundless energy and loves to dance among the flowers, releasing their scent as she pirouettes from bloom to bloom.

Fleur

Fleur is feisty, funny, fiery and cool. Her striking red hair twinkles with tiny stars and her eyes are always changing colour. She loves music and singing. Fleur can make a musical instrument from anything she finds, especially natural things.

Collect them all!

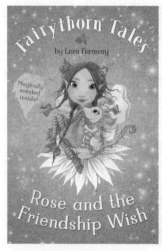

Rose and the
Friendship Wish
ISBN 978-1-84877-968-6

Posy and the
Trouble with Draglings
ISBN 978-1-84877-970-9

Fleur and the
Sunset Chorus
ISBN 978-1-84877-972-3

Honeysuckle
and the Bees
ISBN 978-1-84877-969-3